Building
ON A
Dream

THE
FLATIRON
BUILDING

Nicole K. Orr

PURPLE TOAD
PUBLISHING

Printing   1   2   3   4   5   6   7   8   9

BUILDING ON A DREAM

Big Ben
The Burj Khalifa
The Eiffel Tower
The Empire State Building
Fallingwater
The Flatiron Building
The Golden Gate Bridge
The Great Wall of China
The International Space Station

The Leaning Tower of Pisa
The Louvre
The Space Needle
The Statue of Liberty
The Sydney Opera House
The Taj Mahal
The Trevi Fountain
The White House

Library of Congress Cataloging-in-Publication Data
Orr, Nicole, K.
  Building on a Dream: Flatiron Building / Written by Nicole K. Orr.
    p. cm.
Includes bibliographic references, glossary and index.
ISBN 9781624694356
1. Flatiron Building—Juvenile Literature. 2. New York City, NY—Architecture—Flatiron Building—Juvenile Literature. Series: Building on a Dream: Flatiron Building
F128.8.F55 A44 2019
720.9
Library of Congress Control Number: 2018944206
eBook ISBN: 9781624694349

ABOUT THE AUTHOR: Nicole K. Orr has been writing for as long as she's known how to hold a pen. She's the author of several other titles by Purple Toad Publishing and has won National Novel Writing Month ten times. Orr lives in Portland, Oregon, and camps under the stars whenever she can. When she isn't writing, she's traveling the world or taking road trips. When Orr visited the Flatiron Building in New York City, she didn't think of an iron or an ocean steamer. The building made her think of apple pie, and because that made her hungry, she went and found some.

CONTENTS

The following labels appear on the map:

NEW YORK

Secaucus
Gutte
Union City
Weehawken
STRAWBERRY FIELDS
5TH AVENUE
TIMES SQUARE
ROCKEFELLER CENTER
GRAND CENTRAL TERMINAL
Hoboken
EMPIRE STATE BUILDING
FLATIRON
New York

NEW JERSEY
Bergen

CHINATOWN

NATIONAL SEPTEMBER 11 MUSEUM

STATUE OF LIBERTY

The Flatiron Building sits on a narrow point in downtown Manhattan. In 1912, Taverne Louis opened in its basement. The owners hired jazz musicians from Harlem, bringing jazz to white audiences downtown.

"23 Skidoo!"

When construction crews started working on the Flatiron Building, the people of New York City thought it would surely fall down. Locals and tourists would look up, point at the newest level, and worry. They even made bets. When the building fell, where would the pieces land? Would people or other buildings be damaged?

The area where Broadway, Fifth Avenue, 23rd Street, and 22nd Street come together was a windy place. When the Flatiron Building went up, it funneled the wind and made it stronger. New Yorkers started complaining. Business owners sued the owners of the Flatiron when the wind shattered their shop windows.

New Yorkers believed so strongly that these winds would bring the building down, they stopped calling it by its name. Blaming the architect who had designed it, they called the structure Burnham's Folly. They thought this strange skyscraper was a mistake, and they didn't want it in their city. One 1903 article in the *America Druggist and Pharmaceutical Record* read, ". . . the street passengers are knocked about in all sorts of rude and unkindly fashions, so that it appears as if the Flat Iron Building may not be an unmixed blessing to the locality."[1]

The wind became a problem in other ways.

In the 1880s, a stretch around Broadway came to be called Ladies' Mile. This area, between 15th Street and 24th Street, and from Park Avenue west to Sixth Avenue, was known for its many women's clothing shops. As time went by, other kinds of businesses came to Broadway, but the name stuck. After the Flatiron was built along part of Ladies'

Chapter 1

Women could shop and feel safe on the Ladies' Mile. In the early 1900s, "proper" women were not allowed to go out alone.

Postcards made fun of how windy it was around the Flatiron Building.

Mile, the name made even more sense. When men realized how windy the area was, they started lining up on the corner of 23rd Street. They'd wait for women to walk by the Flatiron Building. When the wind kicked up, the women's skirts would fly into the air. The men would laugh and shout about how exciting it was to see all the ankles along Ladies' Mile. This behavior, of course, was unacceptable. To stop the pranks, police officers would walk circles around the building. Every time they found men sitting on the curb laughing, the officers would chase them away and shout, "Twenty-three skidoo!" This meant, "Leave immediately," and it worked.[2]

Despite the wind and appearances, the building was structurally sound. In fact, building codes had been changed just a few years before to allow for this new type of skyscraper. Called curtain wall construction, it would pave the way for even higher and stronger skyscrapers.

It took a long time for New York to love the Flatiron Building. Now, the Flatiron is as much a part of New York City as the Statue of Liberty.

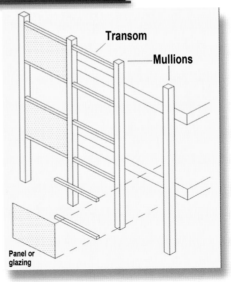

Curtain walls are hung on frames of steel mullions (vertical pieces) and transoms (crosspieces).

The walls of the Flatiron Building look heavy and too thin to stand. The secret? The steel frame, and not the walls, support the building.

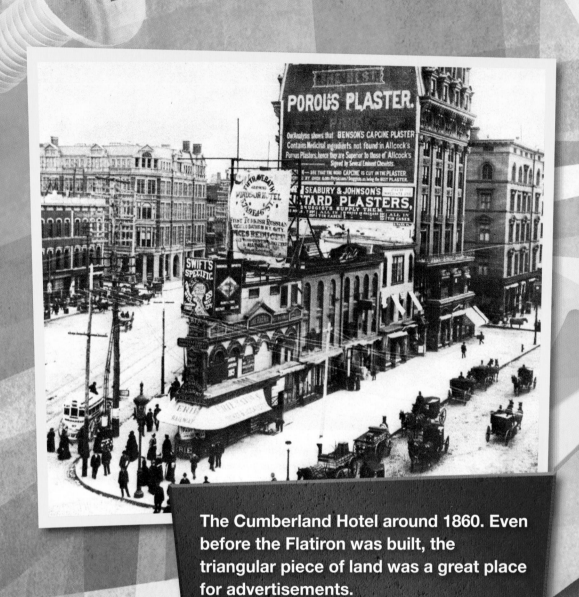

The Cumberland Hotel around 1860. Even before the Flatiron was built, the triangular piece of land was a great place for advertisements.

So Many Buildings in So Little Time

New York City is a very noisy place. It is full of bright lights, famous parks, and celebrities eating in fancy restaurants. People visit the Statue of Liberty, Rockefeller Center, and its world-class museums. In NYC, there are more tourist attractions than one person could see in a month. This has been true of the city for a very long time. Even in 1880, the city was full of famous people and places. But in 1880, the Flatiron Building hadn't yet been built.

The neighborhood where the Flatiron Building stands is called the Flatiron District. That's right! This area was called the Flatiron many years before the Flatiron Building was built. The plot of land on which it stands is in the shape of a slice of pie. This 9,000-square-foot location was popular. Because of how many people passed by each day, it was the perfect space to advertise. It was also the perfect place for businesses. The problem was that no one knew just what kind of businesses should go there.

The first building constructed there was the St. Germaine Hotel. In 1857, Amos Eno bought the land. He tore down the St. Germaine and then built a seven-story apartment building he called the Cumberland. He rented some of the rooms to rich travelers and the rest to advertisers. Eno also put up a large screen on the front of the Cumberland. *The New York Times* and the *New York Tribune* used the screen for news bulletins. On election nights, the screens gave updates to the public.

When Amos Eno passed away in 1899, the lot he'd been managing was sold. It changed hands many times. First, Eno's son William bought

Amos Eno

it. Three weeks later, William sold the property to Samuel and Mott Newhouse. The Newhouses had it for two years before selling it to Harry S. Black. Black was the chief executive officer for the Fuller Company, which specialized in building skyscrapers. Black wanted to build a new headquarters for the Fuller Company, so he brought in two architects. Their names were Daniel Burnham and Frederick Dinkleberg. It was February 1901 when Black offered the two men the job.

Much of the United States already knew Daniel Burnham. He had his own architecture firm in Chicago, Illinois, called D.H. Burnham and Company. Burnham and his firm had designed the National Mall in Washington, D.C. He and Dinkleberg would be a good team too, as they had already designed two buildings together in Chicago.[1]

People laughed at the Flatiron Building both before and during construction. New Yorkers

Daniel Burnham's work helped Chicago recover from the Great Chicago Fire.

worried about the wind and that the structure might fall over. Newspapers and reporters worried that tourists wouldn't appreciate the new skyscraper. Even other architects looked at what Burnham and Dinkleberg were doing and wondered if they were a little crazy.

The Flatiron Building would soon prove all of them wrong.

Burnham's fireproof Masonic Temple in Chicago was one of the first to use a steel frame.

Burnham designed many of the buildings for Chicago's 1893 World's Fair. They featured the Beaux-Arts style that he would bring to the Flatiron Building.

The Great Chicago Fire of 1871 (top) caused massive destruction. Afterward. steel frames were used instead of wood, allowing buildings to be much taller and more fireproof. The Flatiron Building (left) also used steel.

A World of Flatirons

It took a long time to build many of the world's most famous structures. The Statue of Liberty took nine years to build. The Sydney Opera House in Sydney, Australia, took 14 years. The Leaning Tower of Pisa in Italy took an incredible 344 years to be finished. How long did it take to build the Flatiron Building in NYC? Just nine months. This made the Flatiron Building one of the fastest, most smoothly built skyscrapers in New York's history.

New York's Flatiron Building is not the only one of its kind in the United States. In fact, there are more than a dozen other Flatiron Buildings across the country. These buildings can fit into odd-shaped places. There are many cities with small slices of land available. The Flatiron design is perfect for these areas because it is narrow on one end and wide at the other.

When the Flatiron Building was added to the landscape of NYC, it was a relatively new idea. At the time, most skyscrapers were built with thick stone walls on a concrete foundation. Without these heavy walls, tall buildings were at risk of falling down. When Burnham and Dinkleberg were brought on to build NYC's Flatiron Building, they decided to do something different. They used a steel skeleton instead of concrete walls. This was one of the reasons New Yorkers were so afraid the structure would come down. Because of the super strength the steel frame provided, the base could be narrower, the walls could be thinner, and the space inside could be larger. On June 20, 1901, *Life* magazine said, "[But] here in New York the price of land

Lions carved in the Beaux-Arts style adorn the Flatiron.

determines the height of the building and we have to take what comes. All we can do is to hope that it won't be as bad as we fear, and if it is, to look the other way."[1]

D.H. Burnham and Company used ancient architecture in their design plans. When Burnham started work on the Flatiron Building, he was particularly inspired by the Renaissance and the Beaux-Arts style. His designs included a flat roof, as well as arched windows and doors. Almost every inch of the outside would be decorated with murals, statues, and mosaics. Among these plans were a clock face, which was never added, and gargoyles.

The foundation was made of limestone. This strong base would help the Flatiron Building stand against weather and time. The outside of the skyscraper would be made of terracotta. Terracotta is baked ceramic used to decorate the walls of buildings and help make them fireproof.

Just before beginning construction, two more men were brought onto the team: Paul Starrett and Corydon Purdy. Starrett would go on to design New York's Empire State Building. Purdy was a long-time employee of the Fuller Company. Together, Starrett and

Terracotta is durable and flame resistant.

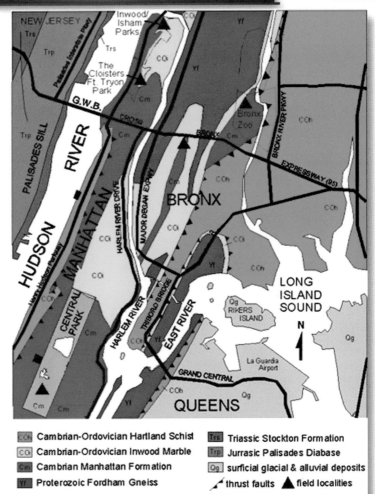

Purdy started ordering materials for the Flatiron Building.

First they reached out to the American Bridge Company and ordered 3,680 tons of steel. Then they ordered concrete, wood, bricks, doors, windows and frames, sinks, and toilets.[2] Besides materials, Starrett and Purdy also needed workers. They contacted countless electrical, plumbing, and elevator companies. They all had to bid on the job. The company that bid the lowest cost and would take the least amount of time would get to work on New York City's newest skyscraper.

Cambrian-Ordovician Hartland Schist
Cambrian-Ordovician Inwood Marble
Cambrian Manhattan Formation
Proterozoic Fordham Gneiss
Triassic Stockton Formation
Jurrasic Palisades Diabase
surficial glacial & alluvial deposits
thrust faults **field localities**

How can Manhattan support so many skyscrapers? Layers of rock give them a firm foundation. In the Flatiron area, this bedrock is about 40 feet below the surface. In the mapped area above, the rock is closer to the surface, so it can support taller buildings.

With the budget for the project set at $1 million, crews could finally knock down the Cumberland and start on the new building. There was just one problem: There was one man still living in the old hotel, and he refused to leave!

The floorplan of the Flatiron Building fits into a right triangle (top). The building is most often photographed from its narrowest angle.

False Starts

By June 1901, crews from the Northwestern Salvage and Wrecking Company had been waiting to start for a month. Colonel Winfield Scott Proskey lived on the sixth floor of the Cumberland. His lease said he could live there until October—so he refused to leave. The Fuller Company offered him large amounts of money to break the lease, but he stayed. Other buildings on the lot were torn down. Proskey's electricity and water were turned off. When the elevators stopped running, Proskey bought a ladder to get to his apartment! It wasn't safe for him to live there anymore, and still he would not leave.

Finally, after the Fuller Company paid most of his debts, Colonel Proskey moved out.[1]

On June 2, 1901, the *New York Herald* featured a picture of Burnham's designs for the building. The caption read, "Flatiron Building."[2] It is strange that the paper called the new structure by this name. Harry S. Black had planned to call it the Fuller Building. Many New Yorkers were still calling it Burnham's Folly. But the name Flatiron stuck. This was the name of the district in which it was built—and the building looked like a flat iron used for pressing clothes.

Even after Proskey moved out, the people working for the Fuller Company weren't able to get started. First, there was a heatwave that lasted more than a week. Some people died from the heat and many others were driven out of the city. Second, Burnham was too busy with other projects to come back to New York City. Third, the original plans for the Flatiron Building were turned down by the Building Department

because of wind and fire concerns. The designs for the structure had to be altered. More professionals were brought in, models were made, and the plans were updated.

Finally, the steel could be brought to the construction site. In New Jersey, the American Bridge Company loaded the steel onto trains. Then the steel was transferred to boats. Once it was across the river, horses pulled the steel to the construction site. The bundles came painted with red numbers so that the crew would know what floor the pieces were for. Two foremen, Dan Dunn and Billy Dell, made sure the steel went where it was supposed to go. They also kept the workers on schedule.

It was January 1902 when the first level of the Flatiron Building was erected. It was just a steel skeleton, and people could see right through it. Construction stopped because of a missing delivery of steel. Then, on February 17, New York was hit with the worst blizzard it had seen since 1888.

More than 15 inches of snow fell on New York City during February 1902. Drifts were as high as five feet.

Once the steel was in place, workers could quickly attach the tiles to make the outer walls.

Once the city recovered from the blizzard, the building went up fast. With a new level of the 20-story structure being built almost every day, crews were both impressing New Yorkers and scaring them. As the crews at the top continued to work on each new floor, crews at the bottom began attaching the yellow-gray terracotta tiles. These arrived in large boxes, packed with straw. Just like the bundles of steel, each tile was numbered.

When the fourth floor was completed, workers began adding decorations. These included sunbursts, buttons, faces, angels, lions, and, of course, gargoyles.

The building was halfway done, but there was a problem. Harry S. Black, who rarely visited the site, wasn't happy. He had paid a very large amount of money for this spot and he did not want to waste a single inch of the space. Black contacted Burnham and told him to change the

Carved faces decorate the 22nd story.

design. Black wanted a section added to the narrow tip of the skyscraper. If this weren't done, the tip of the pie slice would be totally empty. Burnham was angry and told Black in a letter, "There is no way to project these without very seriously injuring the artistic effect of the building. It can be done, of course, but it will be at considerable loss of appearance."[3] Burnham gave in and added a nose to the building made entirely of glass. One story high and just 6.5 feet wide, it would be as strangely shaped as the rest of the structure.

Black pressured the ironworkers, crewmen, foremen, and architects to finish as quickly as possible. He was already putting ads in the paper for people to move in. In October 1902, the Flatiron Building officially opened for business. People could move into the rooms and start eating at the restaurant in the cellar.

The building had 20 levels. In the years following, two more would be added. The 21st, called the penthouse, was added in 1905. People have to use a separate elevator to reach

The penthouse on the tall 21st floor has large windows and extra decoration.

this floor. There, all the windows in the rooms start at the ceiling and come down to chest height. This was done for a better view of the city. A 22nd story was added in 1915.

Later, when asked to describe the Flatiron Building, photographer Alfred Stieglitz said that it "appeared to be moving toward me like the bow of a monster steamer—a picture of a new America still in the making."[4] This was just one of the ways that photographers, architects, reporters, and artists described this skyscraper. It was strange indeed. The side of the building facing Broadway was 190 feet wide. The side facing Fifth Avenue was 173 feet wide, and the side facing 22nd Street was barely 87 feet wide. With these very strange dimensions, how could locals and tourists not look at the Flatiron Building and see irons, ocean steamers, and slices of pie?

Today, with so many other tall buildings around the Flatiron, the wind at street level is not nearly as strong as it was in 1902.

The view from a point office includes the Empire State Building (bottom). The art deco style used in the Empire State can also be seen in the elevators of the Flatiron (top).

Admiring Greatness from Afar

When it comes to the world's most famous buildings, the best way to experience them is by going inside. With the Flatiron Building, choices are limited. If you'd like to visit, you could walk into the lobby and say hello to the security guard at the elevators. You could also visit one of the shops that occupy the bottom floor. Unfortunately, the public isn't allowed to explore the upper levels of the skyscraper, as they are occupied by the publishing house Macmillan.

Don't be too jealous of Macmillan. Having an office in the Flatiron Building might provide amazing views and great bragging rights. However, these offices also have their own set of problems. Because the Flatiron Building is such a strange shape, all the rooms are different sizes. The ones at the narrow end of the building, called "point offices," have angled walls. A desk or bookcase can't be shoved against the wall. With 700 windows and 22 stories, there is no shortage of sunshine. This makes it difficult for people to use computers in their workspaces. Using the restrooms can be a challenge for employees as well. Because restrooms for women were added long after the building was finished, male and female restrooms are on alternating floors.

If not being able to explore all of the Flatiron Building disappoints you, you might be in luck. Macmillan's leases were scheduled to end in 2019, and there was already someone who wanted to move in. Sorgente Group, a real estate investment firm from Rome, planned to make the building into a hotel in 2020.[1]

Many groups of dancers performed at the Flatiron's 110th Anniversary.

The Flatiron Building was having no problem keeping busy while it waited to become a hotel.

On June 21, 2012, a group of dancers celebrated the 110th anniversary of the Flatiron Building. A woman named Shandoah Goldman put together a dance routine called "23 Skidoo." On the day of the celebration, the dancers showed up in evening dresses and performed. While they danced, the wind kicked their skirts into the air. Locals and tourists took endless photos.[2]

Over 100 years have passed since New Yorkers watched the Flatiron Building grow. During that time, little about it has changed. The outside has been cleaned a few times. An angel statue was destroyed and had to be replaced. What has changed, however, are the surroundings. When the Flatiron Building first went up in 1902, it was the only skyscraper in that area of New York. This was one of the reasons it was so windy. More and more skyscrapers have been added over the years. Now the Flatiron Building is protected by the structures around it. People still might have to grab their hats and umbrellas, but the times of high-flying skirts and broken windows are long gone.

The steel frame design that so frightened New Yorkers caught on quickly. It allowed a whole new class of skyscrapers to go higher and higher. Soon, building wars would be waged to see who could build the tallest tower: Manhattan Co., the Chrysler Building, and the Empire State Building vied for the title in the late 1920s and early 1930s.

The Flatiron Building is a great example of how something most New Yorkers hated became the thing they loved. Now this structure is

seen on just as many postcards, paintings, videos, blogs, movies, and selfies as NYC's Statue of Liberty and Freedom Tower. Sure, it might get windy sometimes, and yes, there might be too much sunshine piercing the windows. On the other hand, maybe the thing that isn't perfect is the thing that lasts the longest.

What did Daniel Burnham have to say years after his great NYC skyscraper was finished? "Make no little plans; they have no magic to stir men's blood and probably themselves will not be realized. Make big plans; aim high in hope and work."[3]

Visitors to Madison Square Park can enjoy views of the Flatiron across 23rd Street.

You don't have to travel to New York City to see this amazing structure. In fact, if you'd like to see how well the Flatiron Building and dinosaurs get along, check out the 1998 movie *Godzilla*. It doesn't turn out well for the skyscraper! If you watch the movie *Spiderman: Homecoming*, you can see the Flatiron Building as the headquarters for the newspaper *The Daily Bugle*.

Chronology

1857 Amos Eno buys the St. Germaine Hotel, then tears it down in order to build the Cumberland.

1898 Fuller builds the New York Times Building in Times Square.

1901 Harry S. Black buys the land at 23rd and Broadway for the headquarters of Fuller Company Architects. Once all the residents of the Cumberland move out, the building is torn down. Daniel Burnham and Frederick Dinkleberg then begin work on the Flatiron Building.

1902 The first story of the Flatiron Building is completed. In October, the Flatiron Building officially opens.

1905 The 21st floor is added.

1915 The 22nd floor is added.

1930 New York's Chrysler Building is the tallest building in the United States.

1931 The Empire State Building at 33rd Street and Fifth Avenue becomes the tallest building in the United States.

1972   The World Trade Center in downtown Manhattan becomes the tallest building in the United States.

1974   Chicago's Sears Tower, now called the Willis Tower, takes the tallest building title.

1979   The Flatiron Building is listed on the National Register of Historic Places.

1989   The Flatiron Building is named a U.S. National Historic Landmark.

1999   The hydraulic elevators in the Flatiron Building are replaced with computerized elevators. They are the last of the "water bugs" in New York City.

2012   A flashmob performs at the Flatiron Building.

2019   The leases of the publishing house Macmillan are scheduled to end.

2020   A real estate investment firm from Europe, Sorgente Group, is scheduled to take over the Flatiron Building and turn it into a hotel.

Chapter 1

1. "The 1902 Flatiron Building—23rd Street Between Broadway and 5th Avenue." *Dayton in Manhattan*, June 24, 2011. http://daytoninmanhattan.blogspot.com/2011/06/1902-flatiron-building-23rd-street.html
2. Holland, Evangeline. "The Flatiron Building and 23 Skidoo." *Edwardian Promenade*, November 19, 2013. http://www.edwardianpromenade.com/new-york-city/the-flatiron-building-and-23-skidoo/

Chapter 2

1. Dobbins, Jeff. "The Flatiron Building: A New York Icon." *Walks of New York*, February 18, 2015. https://www.walksofnewyork.com/blog/flatiron-building-new-york

Chapter 3

1. Alexiou, Alice Sparberg. *The Flatiron: The New York Landmark and the Incomparable City that Arose with It*. New York: Thomas Dunne Books, 2010.
2. Grigonis, Richard, "The Flatiron Building, New York City." *Interesting America*, January 3, 2011. http://www.interestingamerica.com/2011-01-03_Flatiron_Building_New_York_by_R_Grigonis.html

Chapter 4

1. Alexiou, Alice Sparberg. *The Flatiron: The New York Landmark and the Incomparable City that Arose with It*. New York: Thomas Dunne Books, 2010.
2. Ibid.
3. Ibid.
4. Ibid.

Chapter 5

1. "Flatiron Building Going Italian: Foreign Investors Buy Majority Stake in 22-Story Building." *NBC New York*, July 16, 2009. http://www.nbcnewyork.com/news/local/Italian-Investor-Buys-Majority-Stake-in-Flatiron-Building.html
2. "Kicking Up Our Skirts for the 23 Skidoo Flatiron Flashmobesque." *Hanky Panky*, June 22, 2012. http://blog.hankypanky.com/23skidoo/
3. Alexiou, Alice Sparberg. *The Flatiron: The New York Landmark and the Incomparable City that Arose with It*. New York: Thomas Dunne Books, 2010.

Books

Beck, Barbara. *The Future Architect's Handbook*. Atglen, PA: Schiffer Publishing, 2014.

Cornille, Didier. *Skyscrapers: An Introduction to Skyscrapers and Their Architects*. New York: Princeton Architectural Press, 2014.

Dillon, Patrick, and Stephen Biesty. *The Story of Buildings: From the Pyramids to the Sydney Opera House*. Somerville, MA: Candlewick Press, 2014.

Mansfield, Andy. *Pop-Up New York*. Melbourne, Australia: Lonely Planet Kids, 2016.

Staton, Hilarie. *Dropping In On . . . New York City*. Vero Beach, FL: Rourke Educational Media, 2016.

Works Consulted

Alexiou, Alice Sparberg. *The Flatiron: The New York Landmark and the Incomparable City that Arose with It*. New York: Thomas Dunne Books, 2010.

Andrews, Evan. "Ten Surprising Facts About the Empire State Building." History.com, April 29, 2016. http://www.history.com/news/history-lists/10-surprising-facts-about-the-empire-state-building

New-York Historical Society Museum & Library. http://www.nyhistory.org

Schons, Mary. "The Chicago Fire of 1871 and the 'Great Rebuilding.' " *National Geographic*, January 25, 2011. https://www.nationalgeographic.org/news/chicago-fire-1871-and-great-rebuilding/

Solomon, Nancy (editor). *Architecture INTL: Celebrating the Past, Designing the Future*. New York: Visual Reference Publications, 2008.

On the Internet

The Flatiron District: The Flatiron Building
http://www.flatirondistrict.nyc/discover-flatiron/flatiron-history/13/the-flatiron-building

History: Flatiron Building
http://www.history.com/topics/flatiron-building

PBS: Treasures of New York: The Flatiron Building
http://www.pbs.org/video/treasures-new-york-treasures-new-york-flatiron-building/

Walks of New York: Flatiron Building
https://www.walksofnewyork.com/blog/flatiron-building-new-york

The Flatiron was the start of the official Sightseeing Tour of New York City for many years.

advertise (AD-ver-tyz)—To use signs, print media, television, radio, or social media to promote a product or idea.

art deco (ART DEH-koh)—A design style of the 1920s and 1930s that featured geometric designs and a combination of old and new materials (such as metal and plastic).

Beaux-Arts (boh-ZAR)—Fine arts; referring to the classical style of art, such as using columns and massive carvings in the style of ancient Greece or Rome.

celebrity (seh-LEB-rih-tee)—A famous person.

ceramic (ser-AM-ik)—Clay that has been hardened using heat.

foreman (FOR-min)—The person who directs a crew.

debt (DET)—Money or payment owed.

election (ee-LEK-shun)—The process by which a person is voted into office.

folly (FAH-lee)—Foolish actions; an expensive mistake.

landscape (LAND-skayp)—The layout of the land; the features of a piece of land.

lease (LEESE)—A contract between an owner and a renter that outlines what property is being rented, for how long, and for what cost.

mosaic (moh-ZAY-ik)—A picture or pattern made using small pieces of a hard material such as tile or glass.

mullion (MUL-yun)—A vertical piece of framework that separates windows or doors.

mural (MYUR-ul)—A large piece of art painted onto a wall or ceiling.

Renaissance (REH-neh-zahntz)—The period in Europe between the 14th and 16th centuries when there was increased interest in the art and writing of ancient Greece and Rome.

transom (TRAN-sum)—A crosspiece in the framework of a wall, especially over a door or window.

CONTENTS

MY AROUND-THE-WORLD ADVENTURE

CHAPTER ONE

On November 14, 1889, I boarded the *Augusta Victoria* in New Jersey. The sun was shining, the sky was crystal clear, and the sea was calm. It was the perfect day to start my round-the-world adventure.[1]

It took seven days to cross the Atlantic Ocean from New Jersey to London. At first I got really seasick. I had never been on a ship before, so it took me a while to get used to it. Once I did, though, I never got sick again for the entire trip.[2]

I arrived in London on November 21. I toured the city for a day, then dashed off to France to meet the author Jules Verne. His book *Around the World in 80 Days* had inspired my trip. He and his wife showed me a map on their wall that compared my route with the route of his character Phileas Fogg. Verne said, "If you do it in 79 days, I shall applaud you with both hands."[3]

WE BUILT THIS CITY

LOS ANGELES

Philip Wolny

PURPLE TOAD
PUBLISHING

PURPLE TOAD
PUBLISHING

Printing   1   2   3   4   5   6   7   8   9

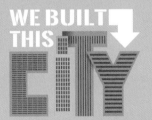

BOSTON

CHICAGO

LOS ANGELES

NEW YORK

PHILADELPHIA

Library of Congress Cataloging-in-Publication Data
Wolny, Philip.
   We Built this City: Los Angeles / Written by Philip Wolney.
     p. cm.
Includes bibliographic references, glossary, and index.
ISBN 9781624694165
 1. United States Local History—Los Angeles – Juvenile Literature. 2. Cities—Urban—Geography—Juvenile Literature. I. Series: We Built this City: Los Angeles.
 F869.A45.GF125 2019
 917.94

Library of Congress Control Number: 2018943947

eBook ISBN: 9781624694158

ABOUT THE AUTHOR: Philip Wolny is an author and editor born in Poland, and has lived in New York City on and off since the age of four. His nonfiction titles for young-adult readers include books about U.S history, international politics, culture, religion, and many other topics. He lived in several neighborhoods of Los Angeles in the early to mid-2000s, including Los Feliz, Koreatown, and the Fairfax District, and remains a big booster of the city.

CONTENTS

Top: Hikers take a break behind the Hollywood Sign. Bottom: A view of the famous sign from below, in the neighborhood after which it was named.

A CITY
IS BORN

In the Hollywood Hills of Los Angeles, California, stands Mount Lee. Near the top of the 1,708-foot-high peak sits the world-famous Hollywood Sign. It has appeared in countless images, films, and television shows over the years. More recently, it has been the background for just as many smartphone selfies, taken by visitors from all over the world. If you stand behind the sign and look around, you can take in many sights that make "the City of Angels" one of the most famous and incredible metropolises in the world.

From the sign, you can see well-known neighborhoods such as the longtime entertainment capital of Hollywood, the soaring towers of downtown Los Angeles, as well as the busy neighborhoods famous for immigrants' contributions, like Mexican-American Boyle Heights and Koreatown. On a clear day, you can see Venice and Santa Monica bordering the Pacific Ocean, and the mountain ranges that surround the city.

However, rewind about two hundred years. You would see a peaceful, empty landscape. Instead of city blocks going on for miles upon miles, skyscrapers, and freeways moving millions, there were thousands of acres of wetlands, forests, meadows, and other natural areas.

The Hollywood Sign has long been a symbol of the glitz and glamour of Los Angeles. But when you look at the huge, sprawling city from the top of the hill, ask yourself: "Who built these neighborhoods?

Narcisa Higuera, later known as Mrs. James V. Rosemeyre, was one of the last Tongva speakers.

Whose hands moved the billions of tons of materials to create the buildings, roads, parks, mansions, and other L.A. sights?"

The answer is: Everyday people, many of them from places like Mexico, China, Korea, Thailand, Japan, Europe, Armenia, Iran, and Russia. As much as any city, Los Angeles was built by immigrants, many of them poor, who had to fight for their rights as newcomers and citizens.

Before any other people lived in what is now Los Angeles, it was occupied by the indigenous people—that is, the people who originally settled there. They lived in the Los Angeles area for thousands of years before Europeans "discovered" North America, much less California itself.

A main people who lived in the greater Los Angeles area were the Tongva. They had neighbors, too, called the Tataviam. They lived in what is now northwest Los Angeles County and the southern part of Ventura County.

When grouped with some of their neighbors, the Tongva were estimated to number about 5,000 in the region as of about 1770.[1] They built villages in the protected bay areas of the Pacific coast, and also alongside the streams and rivers in inland areas. Their land was some of the most fertile in the area. The Tongva were richer and more advanced than their neighbors, and influenced them in matters such as religion.

Imagine now—that instead of shining skyscrapers, parking lots, and apartment complexes—that you are transported to the Los Angeles area of this time. You could walk miles without seeing a soul.

A Tongva *ki'i, or* home

If you stumbled on a Tongva village, you would encounter their domed homes, called *ki'i*. The Tongva placed wooden poles in the earth in a circle, and bent these to meet in the center. They would cover the frames with ferns or, more often, with reeds. The reeds were the leaves of the tule (*TOO-lee*) plant, which grew in the wetlands. They were also used to make boats and mats to sleep or sit on. Sometimes the Tongva would finish the roofs with mats of tule.

Their homes could fit up to sixty people, and three to four families would often live together. A typical village would have anywhere from fifty to two hundred people, according to early Spanish records.

The Tongva and their neighbors gathered acorns and plants, hunted animals and birds, and caught fish, sea lions, whales, and other sea creatures. They also made baskets, ceremonial artifacts, carvings, beads, and other artworks, many of which they used to trade with their neighbors. The area in which this small population lived—the Los Angeles area of the time—was more or less a wilderness compared to today.

The old sacred springs of the Tongva are now known as the Serra Springs, named for the Spanish missionary.

7

By 1829, Mission San Gabriel Arcángelwas raising thousands of sheep and cattle. It also had one of the largest vineyards in Spanish California.

Junípero Serra is celebrated by Americans and Spaniards for his missionary work. Many indigenous people argue that he did as much bad as good.

THE FIRST
ANGELENOS

The world the Tongva had known for hundreds of years would soon change in a big way. In the 1760s, Spanish colonizers arrived. They were led mainly by Roman Catholic missionaries—Spanish people who wanted to convert the Tongva people to their religion. Among the first and most famous structures they built was the Mission San Gabriel Arcángel. Founded in 1771 by Spaniards belonging to the Catholic religious order of the Franciscans, it was built in what is now modern-day Rosemead. This mission was moved to San Gabriel a few years later.

When Spanish colonizers first built settlements in 1769, they called the Tongva people the Gabrielinos (or Gabrieleños), because they were close to the San Gabriel mission. This went along with the Spanish tradition of naming native peoples after Spanish settlements. For example, the Spanish referred to the Tongva's northern neighbors, the Tataviam, as Fernandeños, because they lived near the Mission San Fernando Rey de España. This mission was founded in 1797 in the San Fernando Valley in what is now the suburb of Mission Hills.

The Spanish founded twenty-one missions throughout California in this era. A major leader in colonizing the region was Father Junípero Serra, a Franciscan priest. He started nine of these missions, including the one in San Gabriel.

Like other California tribes, the Tongva and their neighbors were forced to live on the new territories run by the Spanish missionaries.

Chapter 2

Native Americans plow fields near the Mission San Diego de Alcalá.

Those who were relocated were forced to give up their culture, language, religion, and traditions. Instead, they worked on raising European crops and livestock. Though accounts vary, many historians agree that many of these people were treated little better than slaves for the newcomers. Those who refused or fought back were often punished or killed. Diseases brought by the Europeans likely killed the most people, however. Their population dwindled, and few signs of their original culture remain in Los Angeles.

The first eleven settler families—forty-four Spanish subjects from Mexico—formed a town, or pueblo, in 1781. Led by California Governor Felipe de Neve, it was called the Village of the Queen of the Angels ("El Pueblo de la Reina de los Angeles"). The name was later shortened to Los Angeles.

Pueblos were one of three kinds of settlements that the Spanish built in the New World. Pueblos were civilian towns, while missions were run by the church. The third type, *presidios*, or forts, were military bases of the Spanish Empire. For all intents and purposes, the Spanish residents of the Pueblo de Los Angeles could be considered among L.A.'s very first immigrants. Many of them worked on large areas of land called *ranchos* (ranches), where they raised sheep and cattle for the wealthier landowners.

The pueblo of Los Angeles is shown circa 1869, with La Placita Church at the far left.

The newcomers, called *pobladores* (Spanish for "settlers"), were not simply of Spanish descent. Many were of mixed heritage, often partly African and partly Spanish, hailing from the Mexican state of Sinaloa. Mestizos—those of mixed Spanish and indigenous Mexican heritage—would flock to the region in the coming decades.

Because of these changes, the landscape of L.A.'s previous thousand years or so began to change, too. Spanish-style colonial buildings took over the *ki'i*-dotted landscape of the Tongva and others. Churches, walled towns, and other structures like those in Spanish cities back home became a common sight.

In the nineteenth century, California and other parts of the West experienced even greater cultural change. The Spanish banned trading with most foreigners in the early 1800s, but they allowed ships from the new American nation. White Americans slowly but surely settled in the area, too.

By September 1821, Mexico gained independence from Spain, much like the U.S. had from Great Britain decades before. The area of New Spain was now part of Mexico, and would remain so until mid-century.

Perhaps the oldest house that remains standing in Los Angeles proper is the Avila Adobe. Francisco Avila was the son of Cornelio Avila, one of the original soldiers who took control of the area. Francisco and his family arrived in the pueblo when he was two. He went on to become a rancher and one-time mayor of the pueblo. In 1818, he built a house on Olvera Street from adobe, a common building material of sun-dried clay brick. The house still stands in the historic district of Downtown Los Angeles.

The kitchen in the Avila Adobe

Top: Chinese men walk in the city's Chinatown. Bottom: Women walking through Chinatown, sometime around 1900.

A CITY
EXPANDS

The middle of the nineteenth century was one of great change for both the United States and Mexico. From 1846 to 1848, the two nations faced off in the Mexican-American War. The U.S. victory gave it large sections of formerly Mexican land in the West, including California and several other states. A gold rush in 1849 brought as many as 300,000 settlers from other parts of the United States, mostly to the northern part of the state. However, the first discovery of gold in California was actually in Placerita Canyon, just north of Los Angeles, in 1848. The news started a small local population boom. Many came for gold, of course, but others settled in the region to mine other metals, including silver and copper.

The Pueblo of Los Angeles expanded during this time, becoming Southern California's biggest town. While its population was only 141 around 1840, by 1850, that number had skyrocketed to 1,610.[1] Mexico's Congress decreed the pueblo a city in 1835. In 1850, it was officially incorporated, which allowed it to collect taxes and elect its own officials.

In the 1850s, Chinese immigrants began to arrive in the city. Many of them found work with the Central Pacific Railroad Company to help construct the nation's first coast-to-coast, or transcontinental, railway. The first neighborhood known as Chinatown sprang up near modern-day Downtown Los Angeles in the late 1800s.

As the population grew in the late nineteenth century, more jobs brought more people. Chinese and other workers did the heavy labor

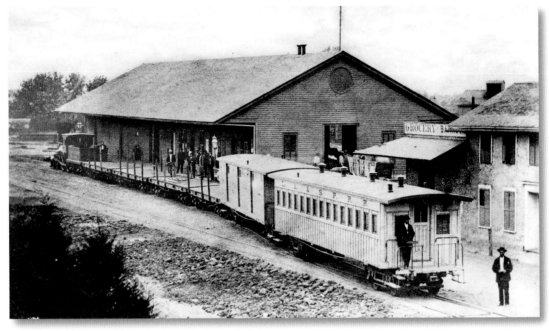

A stop on the Los Angeles and San Pedro Railroad. The transit link helped businesses in the region grow.

required for the 21-mile-long Los Angeles and San Pedro Railroad, built from 1868 to 1869. It connected the growing city with the port town of San Pedro. Older, larger Mexican ranches were divided into smaller farms and plantations. More immigrants, especially from Mexico, tended to fill the jobs of picking crops and performing other types of tough, physical labor.

One of the most important political figures back then was Cristobal Aguilar. He started as a city councilman, and then in 1866 was elected mayor. He set aside public land to create downtown's Pershing Square, a park that remains a popular

A modern park sits at the site of the original Pershing Square.

gathering place. While he was out of office for three months in 1867, Aguilar managed the city's water resources. One of his most important decisions was to refuse, or veto, the sale of the city's waterworks to a private company. Many city historians believe this veto was a main reason the city thrived so well at the time. Aguilar was the city's last Hispanic mayor until the 2005 election of Antonio Villaraigosa.

In 1870, around the time Aguilar won office a second time, the white population of Los Angeles outnumbered Hispanics and Native Americans for the first time. With a great wave of whites settling from other parts of the United States, non-whites were often outvoted in elections, and suffered from unjust and discriminatory laws.

Non-white workers often endured discrimination and violence when they

The original Los Angeles High School is shown in 1873 on Cupcake Hill, at the modern-day intersection of Temple Street and Broadway.

A Chinese worker examines a section of damaged track. In 1867, Chinese immigrant laborers staged the largest strike of the era to fight for better pay and conditions, and to be treated equally compared to whites.

tried to fight for their rights or demand better conditions. They were also often forced by law or custom to live separately from whites, a practice known as segregation. Still, many of them created their own communities, where they preserved their languages and cultures, even as they fought for their full rights as Americans. In the meantime, white Americans soon became the majority not only in Los Angeles, but all across California.

One of the many groups who found ways to thrive and survive on their own terms were newly freed African Americans. After slavery was outlawed in the United States in 1865, a community of several hundred African Americans formed in the city.

Bridget "Biddy" Mason was a former slave who became a nurse, real estate investor, and landowner—one of the first black women to own land in the city. She and her son-in-law, Charles Owens, started a branch of the First African Methodist Episcopal (AME) Church. Using profits from land she owned near downtown, Mason became one of the city's wealthiest and most well known citizens. She learned and spoke fluent Spanish, and she founded a black elementary school and a center to aid travelers.

Biddy Mason lived from 1818 to 1891. She had an amazing journey, from her birth into slavery, to being a pioneer in Colorado and then becoming a rich investor in Los Angeles.

Top: Los Angeles annexed Wilmington and San Pedro as part of the port plan. Center: The city's first oil fields, shown here from 1895 to 1901, were near Toluca Street. Bottom: By 1913, the port had been dredged, allowing even larger ships to use it

OUTWARD AND UPWARD: A WORLD-CLASS CITY

The population of Los Angeles surpassed 100,000 in 1900. Many new developments helped it grow. The discovery of oil in and around Los Angeles and other parts of the state made California the nation's biggest petroleum producer. Oil jobs attracted even more people. Agriculture in the Los Angeles region also brought thousands of newcomers, including new immigrants from Mexico.

Many of them also helped lay more than 1,000 miles of track for the Pacific Electric Company, founded in 1901. By 1920, this company was the world's largest electric railway. It connected distant parts of the region efficiently and cheaply. One of the most important destinations was San Pedro. It was already an important port town when Los Angeles annexed it, creating the new Port of Los Angeles. It became an even bigger center of commerce in the following decades.

Irish immigrant William Mulholland arrived in the city in 1877 at age 22. He was a civil engineer who would head the city's Bureau of Water Works and Supply. From 1907 to 1913, Mulholland led the building of the 233-mile Los Angeles Aqueduct, the biggest in the world then. Without this massive project and the water it provided, Los Angeles would probably not have grown as fast as it did.

Meanwhile, another group of immigrants would change Los Angeles in a wholly different way. Hollywood, about eight miles from Downtown, was originally a sleepy farming town. Instead of the buzz of paparazzi cameras, imagine miles of sunny orange groves. A road between the two was equipped with a streetcar system in 1904—this

Orange groves, like these in Southern California, were one of the main forms of land use in the area. Now, much of the region is highly developed.

would one day become Hollywood Boulevard. Hollywood residents voted to have Los Angeles annex their town because of the bigger city's new and advanced water supply.

The first movie studio in Hollywood, the Christie Film Company, was started by brothers Al and Charles Christie, who moved there from Ontario, Canada, in 1911. Other famous immigrants who helped build the early film industry were Jews from Eastern and Central Europe. Among them were Polish-born Samuel Goldwyn (born Szmuel Gelbfisz), founder of Goldwyn pictures, and Belarusian-born Louis B. Mayer. They co-founded Metro-Goldwyn-Mayer (MGM)

Metro-Goldwyn-Mayer (MGM) Studios in 1916, This production company was located not in Hollywood but in Culver City, which is now a separate city surrounded by Los Angeles.

Studios with Marcus Loew. Loew was the New York City–born son of Jewish immigrants from Austria and Germany. He would also start the Loews theater business.

By the mid-twentieth century, Los Angeles had expanded into a world-famous and world-class city. The freeways connected distant areas with downtown and the beach areas. So did its streetcar system, which automobiles would soon replace. The first skyscrapers included the thirty-two-story Los Angeles City Hall, built in 1928. Very tall buildings were not allowed by the city until voters decided to loosen the rules in 1957. The first new high-rise was the 42-story Union Bank building, built in 1967. A race to build more skyscrapers occurred soon after, and the city's skyline was forever changed. Los Angeles was

The Wilshire Grand Hotel shortly before it was finished.

moving upward as well as outward. As of its 2017 completion, the Wilshire Grand was the tallest building downtown (and in California), at 1,100 feet.[1]

When a city is big enough, it can support major sports teams. Angelenos are proud of their teams, and their venues have become iconic landmarks. Los Angeles Memorial Stadium was opened in 1921. It hosted the Summer Olympics twice, in 1932 and 1984, and has been home base for the Los Angeles Rams NFL franchise, as well as the University of Southern California's (USC) Trojans college football squad. Meanwhile, the Los Angeles Forum in the Inglewood district was headquarters to both the Los Angeles Lakers and Clippers basketball teams until both found a home at the Staples Center in Downtown, which opened in 1999.

The Capitol Records Building resembles a stack of vinyl records and is a Hollywood landmark.

Dodger Stadium, just north of downtown Los Angeles, has become a landmark of the city, and a point of pride for its many baseball fans.

When baseball's Brooklyn Dodgers moved to Los Angeles, the city needed a stadium for them. Eventually, the Chavez Ravine area north of downtown was selected as a site. "They literally moved mountains" to build the stadium, wrote Nathan Masters for KCET radio.[2] Workers moved eight million cubic yards of rock and earth to make room. Opened in 1962, the 56,000-seat home of the L.A. Dodgers remains the biggest professional baseball venue in the world.

Top: Two musicians use a piano to test the acoustics on the grounds where L.A.'s famous music outdoor venue, the Hollywood Bowl, would be built. Center: The Hollywood Bowl in the modern era. Bottom: The venue in 1922.

LOS ANGELES INTO THE TWENTY-FIRST CENTURY

Well into the twenty-first century, Los Angeles has continued to grow and flourish. Long known for its highways, Los Angeles has invested millions in building up its transit system in the last few decades, especially its railways. In 1990, after many years without a true rail line, Los Angeles opened the Blue Line, connecting Downtown with Long Beach 22 miles away. Since then, five other lines have been built or relaunched to help connect the city, using about 105 miles of rail.[1] Many who lived there were happy, because it eased the terribly slow freeway and street traffic. Many more miles of rail were to be built in the next decade, to prepare for when Los Angeles next hosts the Summer Olympics in 2028.

While directors shoot all over the United States, television and film are still one of L.A.'s most important industries. Music and other types of entertainment are also big industries. Every year, thousands of newcomers arrive to try to become stars, or to work in the many jobs that support the entertainment industry. Many more visit to take tours and fill audiences at places like CBS Television City in the Fairfax neighborhood, and at the combination theme park and production facility at Universal Studios.

As many as 47 million visitors flock to L.A. yearly, making tourism big business.[2] Besides its beaches, hiking, food, and nightlife, the arts and culture scenes have attracted painters, sculptors, and other artists to open studios. The Los Angeles County Museum of Art (LACMA),

J. Paul Getty

Museum of Contemporary Art, and the J. Paul Getty Museum are just some of dozens of famous art destinations.

The streets of the city provide their own history lessons. When exploring L.A., you will often encounter the names of famous residents who helped build the city, or had an impact on it. Some of the names are remembered in major streets and roads, or on landmark buildings and structures. The J. Paul Getty Museum was named after and financed by the fortune of the Getty family, whose oil business was once among the world's largest. William Mulholland has the famous Mulholland Drive named after him, as well as a dam and a middle school. Doheny Drive is named after another famous local oil tycoon, Edward L. Doheny. Wilshire Boulevard bears the name of Henry Gaylord Wilshire,

William Mullholland

who was not only a real estate developer, but also a socialist publisher and aspiring politician. This colorful character named the street for himself.

Social struggle and progressive politics are also reflected in L.A.'s street grid. In the 1960s and 1970s, Mexican-American labor activists Cesar Chavez and Dolores Huerta drew world attention by leading the United Farm Workers to protest unfair working conditions and pay. Huerta has had numerous schools named after

Cesar Chavez

Hollywood (foreground), with Downtown Los Angeles in the back

her. Cesar Chavez Avenue runs a few miles through Downtown, and is one of several major streets named after Chavez throughout the world.

Los Angeles might look dramatically different in a couple of decades. There are plans to build new parkland—called "cap parks"—over several major sections of the city's freeways. One plan, called Park 101, would cover some of the 101 freeway extending through parts of Downtown. City planners and others also want to create new green space to run alongside the Los Angeles River. This famous concrete-lined waterway has been featured in dozens of movies, including the Terminator and Transformers franchises.

Although immigration and even birth rates are lower nowadays, Los Angeles's population hit the 4 million mark in 2016, according to the California Department of Finance.[3] Meanwhile, it was only in the twenty-first century that non-Hispanic whites actually became a minority in Los Angeles, a trend that will likely continue for some time. However it changes, Los Angeles will continue to be a cutting-edge, pioneering city for a long time to come.

BCE   The Tongva settle in what will be California. Other nations eventually settle as well, including the Chumash, Kitanemuk, Serrano, and Tataviam.

CE

1771   The Mission San Gabriel Arcángel is established by Father Junípero Serra.

1781   El Pueblo Sobre el Rio de Nuestra Señora la Reina de los Angeles del Río de Porciúncula is founded on a riverside, the first civilian settlement in Los Angeles.

1821   Mexico becomes independent from Spain. Its territories include California and other large parts of the West.

1848   The United States declares victory in the Mexican-American War. It takes over Los Angeles, making all Angelenos U.S. citizens. Gold is found in Placerita Canyon.

1865   Slavery is abolished. Several thousand newly freed African Americans move to Los Angeles.

1869   The Los Angeles and San Pedro is Southern California's first railway, running 21 miles to connect Downtown with San Pedro Bay.

1870   The white population of Los Angeles exceeds the population of Latinos and Native Americans for the first time.

1872   Biddy Mason establishes a branch of the First African Methodist Episcopal Church in Los Angeles.

1873   The city launches its first trolley system.

1880   The University of Southern California is founded.

1900   The population surpasses 100,000.

1913   The Los Angeles Aqueduct is built under the leadership of William Mulholland. It helps secure the city's water supply for many generations to come.

1915   Several large sections of the San Fernando Valley become part of Los Angeles proper.

1909   The city annexes Wilmington and San Pedro. Work begins on the Port of Los Angeles.

1920   Pacific Electric Company becomes the largest electric railway in the country.

1932   Los Angeles hosts the Summer Olympics for the first time.

1939   Union Station, a major transit hub, is opened in downtown Los Angeles.

1962   Dodger Stadium opens.

1973   Tom Bradley becomes mayor. He is only the second African American mayor in a major U.S. city.

CHRONOLOGY

1980   The population passes more than 3 million people. Los Angeles passes Chicago, Illinois, to become the second most populous city in the nation, after New York City.

1984   Los Angeles again hosts the Olympic Games.

1990   The Los Angeles Metro Blue Line opens.

2005   Antonio Villaraigosa becomes the first Latino mayor of Los Angeles in 133 years.

2016   The population of Los Angeles hits 4 million for the first time.

2018   The Los Angeles Philharmonic celebrates one hundred years with its 2018–2019 season.

2028   Los Angeles is scheduled to host the Olympic Games for the third time in its history.

CHAPTER NOTES

Chapter 1. A City Is Born
1. William McCawley, *The First Angelinos: The Gabrielino Indians of Los Angeles* (Banning, CA: Malki Museum Press; and Novato, CA: Ballena Press, 1996), p. 25.

Chapter 3. The City Expands
1   Los Angeles Almanac, http://www.laalmanac.com/index.php.

Chapter 4. Outward and Upward: A World-Class City
1. Matthew Au, "A Brief History of Los Angeles' Tallest Buildings," KCET, February 11, 2014, https://www.kcet.org/shows/artbound/a-brief-history-of-los-angeles-tallest-buildings.
2. Nathan Masters, "They Moved Mountains to Build Dodger Stadium," KCET, October 11, 2013, https://www.kcet.org/shows/lost-la/they-moved-mountains-to-build-dodger-stadium.

Chapter 5. Los Angeles into the Twenty-first Century
1. L.A. Metro, "Facts at a Glance," https://www.metro.net/news/facts-glance.
2. Discoverlosangeles.com, "Los Angeles Welcomes a Record 47.3 Million Visitors in 2016." https://www.discoverlosangeles.com/blog/los-angeles-welcomed-record-47-million-visitors-2016
3. California Department of Finance, ""New Demographic Report Shows California Population Nearing 40 Million Mark with Growth of 309,000 in 2017," May 1, 2018, http://www.dof.ca.gov/Forecasting/Demographics/Estimates/e-1/documents/E-1_2018PressRelease.pdf.

Books

Bauer, Marion Dane, and C. B. Canga. *Celebrating California*. Boston: Houghton Mifflin Harcourt, 2013.

Erlic, Lily. *Los Angeles*. Calgary, AB: Weigl, 2017.

Orr, Tamra. *California*. New York: Children's Press/Scholastic, 2014.

Parhad, Elisa. *Los Angeles Is . . .* Petaluma, CA: Cameron Kids/Cameron + Company, 2018.

Tieck, Sarah. *California*. Minneapolis, MN: ABDO Publishing, 2013.

Works Consulted

Davis, Mike. *City of Quartz: Excavating the Future in Los Angeles*. Brooklyn, NY: Verso Books, 2006.

Heimann, Jim. *Los Angeles: Portrait of a City*. Los Angeles, CA: Taschen America, 2009.

McCawley, William. *The First Angelinos: The Gabrielino Indians of Los Angeles*. Banning, CA: Malki Museum Press; and Novato, CA: Ballena Press: 1996.

Stewart, Gail B. *Los Angeles* (Great Cities of the USA). Vero Beach, FL: Rourke Enterprises, 1989.

On the Internet

City of Los Angeles
https://www.lacity.org

County of Los Angeles
https://www.lacounty.gov

Discover Los Angeles
https://www.discoverlosangeles.com

Los Angeles Times
http://www.latimes.com

GLOSSARY

adobe (uh-DOH-bee)—Clay made from natural materials, dried by the sun or other heat source, and made into bricks for building.

annex (AN-eks)—To claim or add another (usually) smaller territory to a larger one.

aqueduct (AK-wuh-dukt)—An above-ground channel built to move water from one place or another.

incorporate (in-KOR-por-ayt)—To give a town, city, or other community the power to elect its own officials.

indigenous (in-DIH-jih-nus)—Coming from, or native to, a place.

mestizo (meh-STEE-zoh)—A person in the New World who was of mixed European and indigenous background.

metropolis (meh-TRAH-pul-lis)—A large, well-populated city.

mission (MIH-shun)—An area claimed by representatives of the Catholic Church and used as a headquarters to convert native people to their religion.

paparazzi (pah-pah-RAHT-zee)—Photographers who follow and photograph celebrities in order to sell the photographs.

plantation (plan-TAY-shun)—A large farm on which crops are grown for profit.

pobladores (pah-blah-DOR-ays)—The Spanish term that means "settlers."

rancho (RON-choh)—The Spanish term for *ranch*, a large farm where the main business is raising cattle or other animals.

segregation (seh-greh-GAY-shun)—The practice of separating people according to their race or some other trait.

socialist (SOH-shuh-list)—A person who believes in a society in which there is no private property.

transcontinental (trans-kon-tih-NEN-tul)—Going from one side of a continent to the other, such as a railroad that connects the east and west coasts of North America.

tule (TOO-lee)—A plant with wide leaves that is native to wetland areas of California.

veto (VEE-toh)—The legal power to reject a decision or law.

INDEX